The Holiday Rat

A N D

The Utmost Mouse

FELICE HOLMAN

The
Holiday
Rat

A N D

The
Utmost
Mouse

ILLUSTRATED BY
Wallace Tripp

W·W·NORTON & COMPANY·INC·
New York

OTHER BOOKS BY FELICE HOLMAN

A Year to Grow
The Cricket Winter
The Blackmail Machine
The Witch on the Corner
Professor Diggins' Dragons
Victoria's Castle
Silently, the Cat, and Miss Theodosia
Elisabeth and the Marsh Mystery
Elisabeth, the Bird Watcher
Elisabeth, the Treasure Hunter

FOR
Patricia and Arthur Travis,
two of Australia's greatest exports.

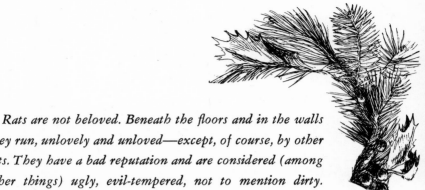

Rats are not beloved. Beneath the floors and in the walls they run, unlovely and unloved—except, of course, by other rats. They have a bad reputation and are considered (among other things) ugly, evil-tempered, not to mention dirty. Above all, they are ordinarily entirely uncelebrated.

And mice! Well, we all know what they say about mice. Timid—that's the main thing. One seldom has heard of an authentic courageous or socially important act of a mouse.

This writer is certainly not going to say that all rats are lovable or worthy of celebration, or that, in their present place in society, all mice are brave. But it is one's wish, if not duty, to call attention to truth, and certain verified events of the last several years do show the unquestionable potential * for lovability in rats, enormous bravery in mice, and for public service in both . . . whether it is a condition that is forced on them or one that they grasp for themselves. These are facts that point to enormous, hopeful possibilities.

* Potential: possibility, what can be—lovability, bravery, and dear knows what else!

The
Holiday
Rat

Mr. Frederick Faithfule the Fourth was sitting fitfully in the factory above the town of Bottome-on-Thames. He had reason to be fitful. The ledger books of the Faithfule Feather-Duster Factory were spread out in front of him in his very chilly office. The brightest thing in the room was the red ink that shone, like Christmas lights, from the

ledger books. Red is a good color at Christmastime, but not in ledger books. It means, to be brief, that things look bad—terrible. Money is not coming in. Indeed, money is all going out—in this case, to pay for repairs to the crumbling factory, to pay old debts for unused feathers, to pay back salaries of employees, coal and electric bills, and on and on. This is why Mr. Faithfule was fitful. Also, it must be said, he had a heart, and a good one at that. He was the fourth Faithfule to

administer the factory, which had been thriving since 1853; and he was the first Faithfule to run right out of red ink.

An old employee named Angus Lowrie put his head into the office. "Mr. Faithfule, sir," he said, "the men in the feather-sorting room are saying that being that their hands are so cold they fumble the feathers, and being as how they have sorted this same lot of feathers twice before. . . ."

"Go home," said Mr. Faithfule. "Tell them,

Angus, they can have the rest of the day off . . . with pay," and he laughed the kind of laugh that tells of no joy.

"What's to happen, Mr. Faithfule?" Angus Lowrie asked, and he asked it timidly because of the lingering habit of old employees of old factories.

"I don't know," said Mr. Faithfule. "Angus, my friend, I don't know. The need for feather dusters seems to be gone. I think we have to open our eyes to that fact, finally."

"I can't understand that, myself," said Angus. "My wife—she couldn't keep house without a feather duster. Poof! The dust is up in the air and away. And they do last! What in the world could have happened?"

"I really don't know and that's the truth," said Mr. Faithfule. "Perhaps dust has declined. Perhaps people have learned to live with dust. Oh, who really knows what makes business boom or wane! I'll confess to you, Angus, that I blame myself.

I am not really a businessman. I am a rose
gardener, at heart, with some slight skill on the
ukulele; and I really would not have taken over
the factory if there had been anyone else to do it."

"Don't blame yourself, Mr. Faithfule," Angus
said. "It could have happened to anyone. But all
the same . . ." and he made a wide gesture that

took in the whole room, the whole factory, the whole town, all the school children and infants, and all the townspeople of Bottom-on-Thames.

"All the same!" cried Mr. Faithfule. *"That's* what is eating me alive! What is to become of the people? And at Christmastime!" And he stopped being fitful and became frantic.

"I'm sorry, sir," said Angus. "I'll tell the men they may go home."

Christmas was twenty days off. The children were already excited. Angus's grandson, John Peter Lowrie, had been searching for his longest sock. He had found it wise to save out the longest one early. If you waited until Christmas Eve, he had discovered, sometimes you couldn't find the really long one. But as he looked through his socks this year, he found that all of them had been mended, and remended, and mended again. And now they were full of holes once more. John Peter and his mother were living with his grandparents

while his father sailed with the British navy.

His grandmother was in the kitchen, looking in the cupboard. It was early enough to be getting together the makings for plum puddings, mince pies, and fruitcakes; but raisins, currants, candied fruits, and nuts are luxuries, and the people of Bottome-on-Thames were not expecting a Christmas of luxuries this year.

"I think perhaps we shall have oatcakes," said the elder Mrs. Lowrie when she had checked the stores in her cupboard. "And I'll just mend that stocking again now, John Peter."

Something like that was going on in nearly every house in Bottome, because except for the milkman, the mailman, and the shopkeeper, nearly everyone in town worked for the Faithfule Feather-Duster Factory, and the word that seemed to be skywritten in that cold December air was: "FINISHED."

John Peter, feeling the mood of the town, was a bit glum, so he ran out of the house to find something to do to cheer himself up. One thing that usually cheered him was throwing pebbles at the rats that lived along the banks of the river—not enough to hurt them, of course, just enough to keep them alert. He was all the way to the riverbank before he remembered. The rats had moved away this winter.

Now *there* was a thing! Of course, when trouble is around and the worst expected, it is natural to

look for signs and omens in everything. And so the people of Bottome-on-Thames took particular notice of the rats. *Was* it or was it *not* significant that the rats, who had always lived normally and peacefully along the banks of the river (where the children could conveniently torment them with pebbles), this winter had moved themselves, for reasons unknown, into the feather factory?

Most of the rats were seldom seen after the move, but one nervy one, perhaps the leader, made a moderate nuisance of himself by tearing into the lunch sacks of the factory workers. It happened often enough to make the carrying of covered lunch pails a wise idea. To Angus Lowrie, he was a particular plague since he had completely chewed up a perfectly good pair of rubber boots that had been left in the cloakroom on a day when it had stopped raining before Angus went home. And *that* rat, called The Rat, didn't mind a mitten or two, either.

When John Peter found himself without any-

thing to throw pebbles at, he thought perhaps he would run away and discover his fortune. But there was hardly time for that because, at five, he had to meet his grandfather Lowrie, as usual, on the path from the factory. Since it was now four-thirty by the clock on the town hall, he decided to walk slowly up the hill.

Before Angus Lowrie went home that day— December fifth, to be exact—he did what he did every cold day of the year. He took his lunch pail and emptied the crumbs and crusts, and occasionally an apple core or a few raisins, onto the hard ground near the side door of the factory. He did this to accommodate the appetites of a family of sparrows that inhabited the eaves on the northeast corner of the building. That family of sparrows and its ancestors had been living there since Angus Lowrie had first come to work as a young boy, and they had never gone hungry. He could say that much.

After Angus had emptied his lunch pail, he followed the rest of the men, who were walking slowly down the steep hill into the town of Bottome, going cheerlessly back to their small, neat homes with nothing hopeful to tell their families.

As soon as Angus had turned his back and the sparrows had snatched a crumb or two, a secret, sneaky sort of thing began to happen. Out of the hole at the bottom of the factory building came The Rat. With a quick look left and right, he dashed across the yard and began to gobble the crumbs and crusts, frightening the sparrows and scattering the birds—first to crisp tree limbs, and then back to their eaves.

John Peter met Angus halfway down the hill
and they walked hand in hand, with John Peter
telling about the oatcakes and the socks, and Angus
not saying anything at all. But after a very few
minutes of walking, something began to nag at
Angus. Had he locked the side door of the factory?
That was his responsibility because he was the
senior employee. Mr. Faithfule, himself, locked the
front door. Angus thought to himself, well, yes,
I did lock it. . . . I think. And then he said aloud,
"All the same, responsibility is responsibility!"
which surprised John Peter since it didn't fit in with
the conversation. "Though who in the world is going to steal anything from a feather-duster factory!" Angus whirled about and started the hard
climb back up the hill. John Peter hurried up to
follow him.

Angus was puffing when he approached the side
door of the factory. And then he saw it: a large,
dark shape licking around the spot where he had

scattered the crumbs. Angus squinted. It was too large to be a sparrow.

"It's a rat! Grandpa, it's a rat!" John Peter yelled, dipping down to find a pebble.

A rat! *The* Rat! The Rat was eating the crumbs Angus had left for his family of sparrows, taking the bread out of their very mouths!

"Thief! Villain!" Angus shouted, running toward the rat and swinging his empty lunch pail in furious, threatening circles. John Peter let loose with his pebble, but it fell far short.

The Rat took a few last licks, drew back on his legs, and, at what seemed a very reckless last moment, sped away at a good clip around the southeast corner of the building, with Angus and John Peter close behind.

"Thief! Villain!" Angus yelled.

"Rat!" shrieked John Peter.

Around the south end of the factory they raced, running hard as they approached the front entrance.

Now, with the kind of precision that only some marvelous design could arrange—or else, some marvelous coincidence—The Rat came abreast of the front door of the factory just as the door flew open, and Mr. Frederick Faithfule the Fourth stepped out. The Rat took it as an invitation, swerved to the right, zipped over the sill of the open doorway, and headed down the dark and narrow corridor.

"Thief! Villain!" shouted Angus.

"Rat!" yelled John Peter.

"What is it Angus?" cried Mr. Faithfule. "What is it?" he repeated, and he grabbed old Angus by the arm as John Peter went tearing past them.

"The Rat, sir! The Rat! He's gone down the corridor there, and there's nothing at the end of it but the cloakroom. I'll get him now!"

"The place is full of rats this year," Mr. Faithfule shouted as Angus pulled away from him and ran down the corridor. "Let him go. At least he hasn't deserted the sinking ship. That's a cheerful sign." But he did not really sound cheerful. He tucked his newspaper, *The Manchester Guardian,* under his arm and stepped back inside the factory. The future beyond the door looked grayer to him than the late afternoon, and now the distress of his old employee upset him. Angus was generally such a steady old soul.

"Thief! Villain! Rat!" came the shouts from the cloakroom, among the empty coat hangers and for-

gotten lunch pails, among the chewed rubber boots
and old raveled mittens, among the broken um-
brellas and torn yellow mackintoshes.

The factory problems must have unsettled
Angus badly, Mr. Faithfule was thinking. And
then, though he was not especially alert for it, out
of the corner of his eye, Mr. Faithfule saw a slight
shadowy motion. The Rat had left the cloakroom
and was in the corridor. Nearly invisible in the

deep and gloomy shadows, he crouched against the wall, making his way slowly towards the door. Mr. Faithfule was not a sportsman, nor a bloodthirsty or violent man. Nevertheless, he reached for the rolled newspaper under his arm, gripped it, took aim, and then, as Angus yelled "Thief!" once more, Mr. Faithfule heaved *The Manchester Guardian* in a magnificent near-miss.

The Rat sped out the front door, rounded the corner of the factory, and dashed down into his hole. The sparrows returned to the remaining crumbs, and Angus emerged, red-eyed and breathless, from the cloakroom, followed by a fairly cheerful John Peter, who had quite worked off his glum feeling.

"Never mind, old friend," said Mr. Faithfule, and he bent to pick up his *Manchester Guardian*. It had unrolled and fanned out into scattered sheets across the corridor.

The last light of day sliced through the doorway and fell on the nearest page like a spotlight. And it was then that Mr. Faithfule froze in his bent-over position. His hand, outstretched to pick up the paper, remained extended, unmoving. His eyes were fixed.

"Angus!" he breathed. Then, "Angus!" he shouted. And then he pointed to the place where the light illuminated the page. It was an advertisement—not large—no, actually quite small, in a

long, long column of advertisements. Mr. Faithfule
read aloud:

WANTED, by Australian importer, factory to
manufacture novelty flowers in large quantities.
Orders will be placed immediately. Call 2131,
Extension 25. Ask for Mr. Chippendale.

"Angus," whispered Mr. Faithfule after a moment, "what does a feather duster make you think of?"

"Dust," Angus replied without hesitation.

"Sneezing," said John Peter.

"No!" Mr. Faithfule ran to the glass sample case in the hallway and grabbed the sample feather duster. "Here, man, hold it! Hold it by it's stem." He pushed the handle of the feather duster, with the feathers uppermost, into the limp hand of old Angus. "Listen, Angus. Stem! Do you understand?" Angus looked suspiciously at the feather duster. "Angus! Friend! Do you hear me, man? Look how the petals droop. *Petals,* Angus!" Angus now looked suspiciously at Mr. Faithfule. Mr. Faithfule rushed on. "Imagine those feathers— petals—in red! Imagine yellow! Blue!"

"Orange," offered John Peter.

Mr. Faithfule patted his head. "Yes, yes!

Orange! Orange *flowers! Feather flowers!* Beauti-
ful, fabulous feather flowers!"

Mr. Faithfule rushed back to his office and
grabbed the telephone. Despite the faulty phone
system of Bottome-on-Thames and its environs, he
got through with only minimal delays to 2131,
extension 25.

"Mr. Chippendale," he said. "Mr. Chippendale, this is Frederick Faithfule the Fourth. I am the proprietor of . . ." and then he took a deep breath, ". . . the Faithfule FEATHER-FLOWER Factory!"

When Mr. Faithfule smiled his way back into the corridor after his long telephone conversation with Mr. Chippendale, Angus Lowrie was still holding the feather duster by its handle—its *stem.* He was watched by a wary John Peter who circled him as if he were a very interesting museum statue.

"Angus, friend, tomorrow you may tell the men to come for their Christmas bonuses."

"Christmas!" exclaimed John Peter.

"Oh Lor!" said Angus.

"Yes, indeed," said Mr. Faithfule.

"That *Manchester Guardian* is a wonderful newspaper," the mailman said the next day. "A wonderful newspaper. I always said so."

"That may be," said Mrs. Lowrie, "but 'twas Mr. Faithfule's wits that did it."

"When you get right down to it," said the head feather-sorter, who was now directing the sorting with an eye to supple shorter feathers suitable for dyeing, "it was Angus feeding them sparrows."

"No!" Angus said. 'It was The Rat!'" and he said it reverently, but he said it firmly.

"It was The Rat all right," was the murmur that went through the feather-sorting room and out the door and into the tying room and out that door and into the packing room and through the office and right through the factory

and

down

the

hill

to   the   schoolhouse,

where John Peter was telling the story for the twenty-seventh time, and through the town where the women were already busy laying down the fruitcakes.

"That's one wonderful rat!" said Angus. "One wonderful rat!"

As far as is known, The Rat was never seen again at the factory, and it wasn't long before John Peter discovered the whole colony back at its riverbank home, just waiting for a good stimulating game of Pebble-Shy. But, over the door of the Faithfule Feather-Flower Factory is a coat of arms—a rat rampant on a field of flowers—with the inscription: THE RAT OF BOTTOME-ON-THAMES. It is an unusual but handsome emblem. It is polished daily. And on December fifth, every year, the town of Bottome-on-Thames

The rat of Bottome-on-Thames

has a special holiday: Rat Holiday. It starts with a ceremonial scattering of breadcrumbs. Then, a testimonial to The Rat is read by Angus Lowrie. An important feature is the school-children's play, a dramatization of the highlights of that memorable day. The first year that it was performed, John Peter was chosen to play the part of The Rat, but after that, it became the custom to allow the best student in the class to have that honor.

After the play, Mr. Faithfule displays his sketches for the new year's line of feather flowers. He tends to favor roses, but he does not overlook such popular and well-loved flowers as petunias, marigolds, and mums. The holiday then moves on to hot cider and a lot of merrymaking all around, while Mr. Faithfule does a few turns on the ukukele before the Christmas bonuses are given out.

Rat Holiday. It is a hopeful day. A wishful and wonderful day.

The Utmost Mouse

The Utmost Mouse

Good heavens! There was a terrible to-do, hub-bub, and brouhaha about the building of the power station. Nearly everyone in Upper Moose was milling around the town with signs.

"NO POWER STATION FOR UPPER MOOSE" was the main message.

"DON'T OVER POWER US." That was a clever one!

The children of the town just loved walking around with signs. They spent a lot of time lettering them.

"GO AWAY, MEAN OLD POWER COMPANY," a fourth-grade boy had written on bright-yellow poster board with brilliant-red crayon.

One big sign made by a first-grader just said, "NO!"

One enterprising schoolboy had a sign that read, "I TAKE ALL MAGAZINE SUBSCRIPTIONS. CALL BILLY. UM-3387." That idea caught on, and soon

there were other business signs. A boy named Omir Obuchowski had a sign that said, "LEAF-RAKING, CHEAP." He didn't get any business—possibly because it was the wrong season—and that was a lucky thing, because otherwise all this might not have happened.

Most of the signs kept to the point, and the point was that while a lot of people thought a new, more-powerful power station sounded like a useful thing to have—to turn on all the lights, run all the electrical equipment, and do all the things that the little, old water-power station did—nobody wanted the power station in his backyard. And no wonder! It was big, for one thing, smog-ugly, for another; and there would be all kinds of wires and cables and things coming out of it and running all over the place to spoil the landscape.

The Mayor of Upper Moose talked to the head of the power company, whose name was The Commander. "We would be very happy to have more electric power, of course," said the Mayor. "But please make it somewhere else. We'll just have to get by with our little old water-power station. We'll manage somehow. Thank you all the same, if you please." He was extra courteous, being a mayor.

It's not easy to push power companies around. They are big, any way you look at them. And powerful. But the power-company officials were going to need the help of the people of Upper Moose if they were to build there. Also, there is something called Public Relations, so they thought twice. Then they thought three times. And it was while they were thinking it over for the fourth time that a very clever, very old man who lived in Upper Moose said to the head of the

power company, "Listen, Commander. I have three-hundred acres upriver, at the north end of town, where nobody lives within sight. I've used it for camping, mostly, but I'm too old for camping now. I'll let you have it for a song if you give up the idea of building in Upper Moose. These people shouldn't have to put up with your smoky towers and big, ugly cables if they'd rather look at the scenery."

So The Commander and the board of directors

of the power company went up the river to look; and they grumbled a lot because it was going to mean extra miles of running wires, and that meant a lot of extra dollar signs with numbers and zeros after them. But then, The Commander pointed out that they would be saving lots of zeros on the land,

because the very clever, very old man was selling the land for a song. So, just to end the to-do, the hubbub, and the brouhaha, they decided to do it.

"Roger!" said The Commander, when it was all decided, although there was no one named Roger around at the time. As a matter of fact, he was addressing the new young engineer of the project, whose name happened to be Jim. "Let's get this thing going fast now," The Commander said to Jim. "Get it off the ground, and get in

touch with me if you run into any hang-ups. Over and out!"

Before the power company had become so big and had been a smallish water-power company, The Commander had been a much milder person. He liked fishing a lot, and he enjoyed going up to watch them build a new dam. He liked to see the waterfalls. Some of them were quite magnificent. He felt, then, that he was turning quiet rivers into roaring falls. But right now, he was building great, silent, smoky buildings that did not make magnificent waterfalls. The Commander stopped fishing, and started wearing an air-force jacket and saying things like "Roger" and "Over." Lately, when the board of directors had been talking about building nuclear-power stations, he had started to say "A-okay," and sometimes he said "Count down," for no particular reason. Everyone called him The Commander because that is what he told them to call him.

It is *humanitarian* when thought is given (by mayors, power companies, rich old men, or whomever) to the real needs and wishes of *people.* Yet, there seems to be no such word as *animalitarian.* So, seemingly because there was no such *word,* there appeared to be no such *thought* or *act,* either, and the power company moved into the three-hundred acres without a thought to the beaver, muskrat, deer, rabbit, fox, and bird families it upset. And mouse!

As soon as the buzz-saws and bulldozers arrived and started to buzz and bull, as soon as the trees started to topple and earth was dug and moved in all directions, animals began to move in all directions too. Abandoning their safe and comfortable homes, where berries and leaves suited their appetites and fresh streams quenched their thirst, deer ran north and deserted the country altogether. Beavers, who had spent goodness-knows-how-many hours building and mending

their complicated dams, sadly went upstream and hopefully began again. Muskrats and foxes followed. Birds watched their nests fall to the ground in trees, and then went away. Rabbits ran to thickets at the edge of the three-hundred acres. Snakes whipped through the grass and woods. Even the beetles, grasshoppers, and crickets moved. And the mice moved. Well, *nearly* all the mice!

Right at the edge of the enormous excavation, nearly in the shadow of the sixty-foot crane, was a mouse family. Despite the fact that all the other mice had left, this family refused to move. Refused? Well, what one means is that they certainly had every chance to move, and so one assumes— one guesses—that they remained out of choice. Perhaps it was simply that the baby mice were too young to travel and the mother had just said something like, "No! Here I stay." Of course, they might just have been stupid and unaware of the

danger. But that is doubtful . . . really doubtful.
It would take an unusally stupid mouse not to
realize that dynamite blasts, steam shovels, a sixty-
foot crane lifting steel girders, not to mention men
in herds, were a real danger. And mice are not
brave . . . usually. But still they stayed safely
enough in a nest that was well protected by a great
boulder, which was being left just where it was,
and would eventually have a copper plaque fixed
to it with the name of The Commander on it.

As the spring came on, and the leaves all burst
in the woods, and the streams fully unfroze, and
the mouse offspring grew, the power station began

to take shape. When the foundations were poured, one could see the great size of the building, and when the crane lifted the steel girders, one could get an idea of the building's height. After a while, its tall chimneys rose above the highest trees.

Omir Obuchowski, finding it the wrong season to rake leaves, used to come upriver to see the work. He loved to watch his father run the big crane. It was like watching a great puzzle being put together. On the days he came to the three-hundred acres, he would watch the different workmen for a while, have lunch with his father, talk to Jim, the nice young engineer, take a swim in the Upper Moose river, fish a little, and generally make quite a vacation of it.

It was during a lunch hour in mid-July, when the young engineer and Mr. Obuchowski and Omir were resting near the big crane, that Omir discovered the little field mouse. He saw him, first, creeping under some leaves near the big boulder where he lived. Then Omir saw him peeking from behind some sticks. He laughed. It is surprising

how loud a laugh can be in the woods during the
quiet of a lunch hour, when men who have been
working hard are lying on their backs, getting the
summer sun. Omir held out a bit of his sandwich to
the mouse. The mouse did not move towards it,
but he did not run away, either.

One does tend to accept what one is accustomed
to, and so this particular mouse, who was one of
those who had been raised in the shadow of a
sixty-foot crane at the base of a power station, ac-
cepted it along with the trees and the grass. And
he also came to accept, as part of his life, the person

of Omir Obuchowski, a young boy with many interests, which had not, until now, included either power stations or mice.

Omir named the field mouse Stanley, and it was not long before Stanley would come out from wherever he was whenever Omir turned up. And then, by and by, it was Stanley, as much as the crane, that lured Omir upriver during the summer days; and after school started, in the late fall afternoons. The attraction must have been mutual because, when the mouse family finally grew up and moved to the edge of the three-hundrd acres, Stanley stayed on.

Omir taught Stanley a number of tricks. Or, perhaps, Stanley taught Omir a number of tricks. However it was, when Omir held out a cooky crumb in his fingers, Stanley would get up on his hind legs and reach for it. If Omir put his hand on the ground, Stanley would climb onto his hand and then up his arm. Then Omir could walk around with Stanley sitting comfortably on his

shoulder, or occasionally on top of his cap. No one
paid much attention to either Omir or Stanley, and
so they paid attention to each other. Sometimes
Stanley would lead Omir through the woods,
playing a sort of Hide-and-Seek, and sometimes, if
they wandered far enough away from the power
station, Omir would catch sight of a deer or a
rabbit and, occasionally, a mouse. And then it oc-
curred to him that except for the birds that passed
overhead on their way from one place to another,
Stanley was the only animal in the three-hundred
acres.

"Why is Stanley the only animal around here?"
Omir asked the nice young engineer, because Jim
seemed to know a great deal. This was Jim's first
chance to be head of a project since he had been
graduated from engineering school, and he was
busy doing his best. He was building the power
station as if he were building the Taj Mahal. Sometimes he even called it "the Taj."

Omir's question seemed to embarrass Jim. He

liked building useful things, but he did not like tearing up the woodlands. "It's all the machinery and the noise," he said a bit brusquely. "It's this enormous building. They never heard and saw this sort of thing before."

"Oh," said Omir. And then he said, "Then, I wonder why Stanley is here?"

"I don't know," said the nice young engineer, and he rushed off to work on an important corner of the Taj Mahal.

Mr. Obuchowski said he didn't know either. "There's probably a reason, but I don't know what it is," he told Omir.

"What are you hanging around here for, Stanley?" asked Omir, but he did not expect an answer. In his experience, animals did not answer questions, no matter how nicely you asked them. He secretly hoped, though, that the answer had something to do with him. There was always the chance that Stanley stuck around because Omir was there, and this may have been the fact.

Every few weeks The Commander would come by, and walk around and around and say, "Hm. It looks A-okay!" And then he would climb into his car, wave to the young engineer named Jim, and yell, "Roger! If you run into any hang-ups, just put a hold on the operation and call me." And then he would zoom off.

But there weren't any hang-ups—at first. And then, towards the very end, it happened! Because, even with the clever young engineer, how could you possibly build a great big thing like a power station, with winter closing in tight, without at least one ordinary hang-up? And this one wasn't ordinary!

It really had been going marvelously. They had had a nice old-fashioned country celebration when the roof was raised, and put a little balsam tree at the top of the building for the traditional rooftree. The construction part was over, and they were running wires and cables. The work of the big crane was really over too, but Mr. Obuchowski stayed around

and pitched in on the stringing of wires and cables.
Some of the wires and cables went overhead, and
that went just fine. No hang-ups. But there were
some big underground cables and they ran through
conduits, which, Omir discovered, was only a fancy
way of saying pipes. First the men put down long
pipes in trenches, and ran cables through the pipes
to the edge of the clearing in the woods. The power
from the power station would be carried through
these cables to wires that would carry the power to
the towns. Well that was more or less the idea as
Omir came to understand it. At first that work went

well, and when The Commander came one day and saw how well everything was going, he said, "I want to dedicate this building on Christmas Eve! Yes, that's what I'll do. It will make very good public relations. I will push a button," he was thinking out loud, "that will set the Upper Moose plant in operation, at the same time lighting the little fir tree on the roof, which you can decorate with Christmas lights. What do you think of that!" But he didn't wait for an answer. "Make sure all the connecting cables are operating by then," he directed the nice young engineer.

Jim, the nice young engineer, nodded, but then he said, "There's only this, Commander. We are running into a little hang-up."

"Hang-up!" cried The Commander, and it seemed he was rather excited about the idea. "What is it?"

"Well," said Jim, "for some reason, we are having trouble running the final cable through the conduit."

"The final cable!" exclaimed The Commander.

"Yes, sir."

"Millions of dollars for a power station!" cried The Commander.

"Yes, sir, or thereabouts," Jim said.

"Technology has advanced to a point where we can send space ships to the moon, and you are not able to run a cable through a conduit?"

The nice young engineer looked sorry that he had told The Commander about the hang-up.

Omir, standing off to the side, found himself humming "Cable through a conduit. Cable through a conduit. A cable isn't able to run through a conduit." Stanley ran up and down Omir's arm excitedly.

"Well, I'm glad you told me about it," said The Commander. "Now, get on to it, and let me know how you make out." And he was off.

'Yes, sir," muttered the young engineer, and he went back to peer into the entrance to the conduit, which he did by lying on his stomach in the

trench. For all his pains, he only got muddy, because he knew perfectly well he couldn't see anything. It was black as a moonless night in a coal mine, inside the conduit. It veered off underground, and then, if he remembered correctly, this particular conduit made a sharp turn halfway through, angling off to the edge of the three-hundred acres. And *that* was probably what the hang-up was, Jim thought. Maybe there was something stuck in that angle. Maybe it was iced up or packed with earth. Maybe it was just that the high-powered machine that pushed the cable through just couldn't manage that angle. Whatever it was, it was a hang-up. For the first time the nice young engineer looked at the Taj Mahal glumly, and it looked like a big, ugly power station.

"The Commander will have my skin," he said. "He sees himself lighting that rooftree on Christmas Eve, and I'm not going to be able to do it. Why didn't I take up surfboarding for a profession!"

The next day The Commander came back with the power company's chief engineer, from the main plant. The chief engineer said that they would just have to get some kind of special machine that knew how to do the job.

"But that will take a while and we'll have to put a hold on this operation!" cried The Commander.

"Affirmative," replied the chief engineer, who spoke the same language as The Commander.

"No!" cried The Commander getting quite fearsome. "I've announced to the press that I will dedicate this building on Christmas Eve. I've told the Mayor and the board of directors. *I* will not be the goat! I want this done by Christmas, and that's that!" and he drove off.

The young engineer was standing in a nearby muddy trench and he kicked the conduit. "Looks like *I'm* the goat," he said.

Omir and Stanley listened to the crisis developing. Jim had stopped kicking the conduit and was talking to some of the men. Sometimes he was serious and sometimes he wasn't. "What I need," Jim said, in a moment of lightheadedness, "is a very small man to run through the pipe and see what the trouble is." All the men laughed because the pipe, it must be remembered, was three-inches wide, and so this was recognized as a joke . . . by most everyone.

Omir did not think it was so funny. He thought about it. And then, while everyone sat around and exchanged ideas about pounds of pressure, and angles of incidence, and articulated joints, and other highly technical stuff, Omir and Stanley wandered over to the conduit. Omir got down on the ground and peered in . . . and then Stanley

got down and peered in . . . and then Stanley looked at Omir, and Omir looked at Stanley.

Now, who is to say with any certainty what is going through an animal's mind and heart at a particular time? All that can be said is what *happened,* and what happened was that Stanley took a few steps into the conduit, and then a few more, and in a minute he was back looking up at Omir. And then Stanley, very purposefully, turned around and went in again and was gone a little longer, and then he came back and looked at Omir. All in a second, Omir scooped up Stanley, only stopping to give him a crumb and a little pat, and dashed over to the group of workers.

"Stanley and I have an idea!" he said. Everyone laughed, except Jim, and he said courteously, "What's your idea, Omir?" perhaps because he was young enough to remember how it felt to have people laugh when you had something to say.

"It's just that I thought—well, it's really

Stanley's idea—that Stanley can go through the conduit."

"Stanley!" said Mr. Obuchowski, with a laugh. "What good would that do, Omir? Stanley can't talk and tell us what the matter is."

But the young engineer jumped up. "No, you're right! He can't *tell* us what the matter is. But, if he could go through. . . . *If* he could go through. . . . Come on!"

Everyone followed Jim down to the entrance of the conduit, and Omir and Stanley were ushered to the spot like royal visitors. Omir felt quite important, though a little nervous.

"Now," said the young engineer, "show me!"

Omir put his hand down to the conduit, and Stanley, first looking all around him and perhaps feeling the importance of the occasion, walked down Omir's arm and into the conduit. All the workers held their breath. Stanley was gone only a few seconds, and then he put his nose out. Omir gave him a cooky crumb. Then, Stanley turned

right around and went back in. He was gone for
nearly a minute. Omir began to get nervous.
"Stanley!" he called through the conduit. Stanley
appeared immediately.

"Give him *two* crumbs!" cried Jim. Omir got
the idea. So did Stanley. He turned around and
went into the conduit again and was gone another
minute or so.

"Stanley!" called Omir. "Stanley, come on out
now." In a few seconds Stanley's nose appeared
at the entrance to the conduit. When he emerged
he was a little muddy. Omir picked him up and
gave him three crumbs and brushed him off.

"That's enough for today," said Jim, looking
happy for the first time in days. "Have that mouse
here first thing in the morning. He's on the pay-
roll."

First thing in the morning on the day before
Christmas, out in the woods, with snow promised,
is a crisp and cold experience, but there was a lot
of excitement to warm things up.

Jim arrived in his jeep with some new equipment. There was a large spool of thread, a ball of twine, a bale of cord, a long length of heavy wire, and then there was a big, white, mysterious box.

Jim didn't lose any time. "The Commander will be here at four o'clock," he said to the men. "Let's blast off! Roger!" Then he hit himself on the side of the head with his hand, "Oh gosh, I'm sorry," he said. "Well, let's just get going, anyway, and see what happens. Come on, Omir. Come on, Stanley."

While Stanley made some trial runs in and out of the conduit, Jim got things ready. He took the

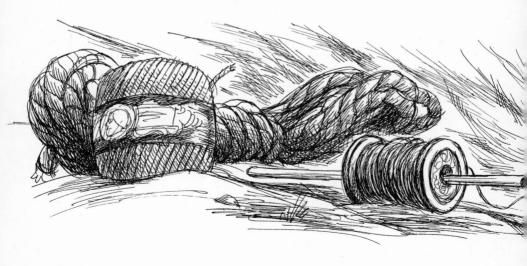

spool of thread and stuck a stick through the hole
so that the spool could turn on it like a wheel.
Then he loosened a length of the thread and went
over to the entrance to the pipe.

"Now, you just tie the end of this thread
around Stanley," Jim said to Omir.

"I don't know if he'll like that," Omir said, and
he looked doubtful. Stanley may very well have
looked doubtful, too. It was hard to tell.

"Try it," Jim said, and he handed the thread to
Omir. Stanley was surprisingly agreeable and

allowed Omir to tie the soft thread around his belly—not too tight—and then Omir put him down at the entrance to the conduit.

"Go on, Stanley!" said the young engineer softly. "Be a brave old mouse and do your utmost. That's the boy!"

Omir said, "Go ahead, Stanley," and then Stanley ran off into the conduit.

"Now!" Jim cried. "Omir, you run around to the far end of the conduit and call Stanley. Quick!"

"I don't know," said Omir. "I'm beginning to be afraid I'll lose him in there. What if there's water in there? What if he get's hurt? What if. . . ."

Jim was impatient. "Everything depends on this, now," he said. "If Stanley's not afraid to do it, you can't be, either. Go on. Run!" And Omir was off and running across the three-hundred acres to the end of the conduit.

In a couple of minutes, Stanley was back at the entrance, looking out expectantly. He stared up at everyone. He looked around. Omir wasn't there. Then through the pipe Omir's voice could be heard faintly. "Stanley. Come on, Stanley." Stanley turned and dodged back into the conduit.

The slack on the thread was used up and the spool on the stick in the young engineer's hand began to unreel . . . ten feet . . . twenty feet . . . thirty . . . as Stanley made his way into the pipe. *And then it stopped.* The young engineer let out an exclamation of disgust.

"Stanley!" Omir called, now quite worried. "Stanley!" The spool moved a bit . . . an inch or two . . . and then another inch . . . and then another . . . and then, suddenly, as Omir called a loud "Stanley!" the spool started to whirr, and you

couldn't count the feet of thread that spun out of the spool, it went so fast. Jim quickly planted the stick holding the spool into the ground, and ran to the other end of the pipe to join Omir. The other men followed. They arrived at the moment that Stanley, moving as if shot from a cannon, ran out of the far end of the pipe and zoomed onto Omir's lap.

"Oh Stanley!" cried Omir, picking up the muddy little mouse and untying the thread.

Jim yelled, "Greetings, you honorable mouse!" and he took the end of the thread and tied it to a nearby pole. Then he ran off, calling the men to bring the rest of the stuff from the jeep.

"So *that's* why he stayed around!" said Mr. Obuchowski. And Omir nodded, as he gave Stanley five crumbs.

After that it was only a few hours' work. They tied the twine to the thread at the entrance to the conduit, and then just kept pulling the thread through the far end until the twine came through. Then they tied the heavier cord to the twine and pulled that through. Then they pulled through the heavy wire. And when they had pulled the heavy wire through, they were ready to draw through the cable.

Laying the first transatlantic cable couldn't have been more celebrated. The cable came through as easily as threading a needle. The electricians pounced on it immediately and made the important connection with the main cable. It was done!

At four o'clock, on the dot, The Commander drove up with the Mayor, the board of directors, a photographer, and a reporter. The Commander seemed in a nervous mood and was heard to mutter, "It had better be lights-on for this plant, or it will be lights-out for *someone* around here!"

The nice young engineer's normal wish to punch The Commander in the nose was blurred by his great sense of success. "It's lights-on, sir," he said.

"Roger!" said The Commander, perking up and stepping grandly over to the switch, which

was now wreathed in holly. And then The Commander pushed the switch, and on the top of the power station the little balsam Christmas tree lit up, signaling that the Upper Moose power station had begun operating. There was a round of applause.

At this point, The Commander started to make a speech. The Mayor listened attentively, though his ears and toes were beginning to get very chilled. The board of directors listened, too. As for the rest of the men, their attention was not entirely on The Commander. Jim, the nice young engineer, had brought the mysterious white box from the jeep and was opening it on a big stump. They all watched as he lifted out a magnificent frosted cake, on the top of which was written, "Stanley, Utmost Mouse." The young engineer grinned at Omir, and Omir came over and put his hand down near the cake. Then Stanley ran down his arm right onto the cake and waited only a polite moment before he dug in.

"Hurrah!" everyone shouted, and The Commander was very pleased because he felt it was in homage to him.

"Roger!" he replied.

"Hurrah!" everyone said again, and Stanley looked up from the cake covered with frosting and pleasure.

"Merry Christmas, men!" cried Jim, the nice young engineer as he climbed into his jeep and turned it towards Florida. "Merry Christmas, Omir! Merry Christmas, Stanley!"

"Merry Christmas, Jim," said Omir as a new snow began to fall on a frosted cake and mouse.